MY FIRST AIRPLANE RIDE

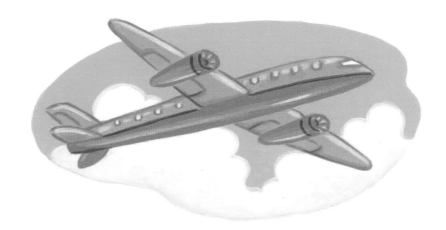

BY PATRICIA HUBBELL
ILLUSTRATED BY NANCY SPEIR

two lions

two lions

Amazon Children's Publishing, P.O. Box 400818, Las Vegas, NV 89140
www.amazon.com/amazonchildrenspublishing

Hubbell, Patricia.
My first airplane ride / by Patricia Hubbell ; [Nancy Speir, illustrator]. — 1st ed.
p. cm.
Summary: Follows a young traveler through a first airplane ride, from takeoff to touchdown.
ISBN 9781477816752
[1. Stories in rhyme. 2. Air travel—Fiction.] I. Speir, Nancy, ill. II. Title.
PZ8.3.H848My 2008
[E]—dc22
2007041979

The illustrations are rendered in acrylic paint on illustration board.
Book and cover design by Becky Terhune
Editor: Margery Cuyler

Printed in China
First edition

FOR SHOSHI, SHIRA, MEGAN—
THREE VETERAN TRAVELERS!
—P.H.

FOR RALPH
—N.S.

Grandma says, "Come visit me!"

Time to go! Lots to see!

Airport ahead. We park our car.

Plane will take us far, far, far!

Go inside for our boarding pass.

Watch the planes through the big plate glass.

Security check. Take off each shoe.

Lift our suitcases. Backpacks, too.

Read the signs. Find our gate.

GATE 18

Play. Talk. Laugh. Wait.

Walk the Jetway. Time to fly!

Soon our plane will be so high!

Aisles. Seats. Luggage rack.

There's a bathroom in the back.

Look around. Find our seats.

Snuggle down. Have some treats.

Attendant tells us what to do.

She's part of the busy crew.

Flying time is almost here.

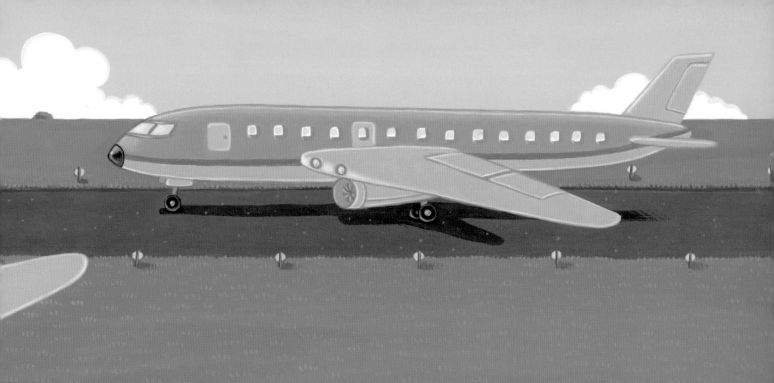

We'll take off when the runway's clear.

Air controller says, "Okay!"

Plane taxis. We're on our way!

LIFTING! Whooshing! **CRUISING!** Soaring!

SHUDDERING! Shaking! **RUMBLING!** Roaring!

Watch a movie. Read a book.

Out the window—Look! Look!

Forest. Lake. Highway. Town.

Earth's so small as we look down.

Here's a pillow. Time for naps.

Teddy bears snooze on our laps.

What a long, exciting day!

Time to land. Airport below!

Wheels touch down. Get set. . . . Let's go!

Back through the Jetway. Hurry! Ohhh . . .

Grandma's waving! Hug hello!

PATRICIA HUBBELL has written a number of lively books about things that go, including *Airplanes: Soaring! Diving! Turning!*, *Cars: Rushing! Honking! Zooming!*, *Trains: Steaming! Pulling! Huffing!*, and *Trucks: Whizz! Zoom! Rumble!* She lives in Easton, Connecticut. To find out more about Patricia Hubbell, visit www.kidspoet.com.

NANCY SPEIR has worked as a commercial artist, designer, and children's book illustrator. She recently illustrated *Eliza's Kindergarten Surprise* by Alice B. McGinty. She lives in Santa Rosa, California.